The CAT WHO WANTED to FLY

Written by Robyn Supraner
Illustrated by Joan E. Goodman

Troll Associates

Library of Congress Cataloging in Publication Data

Supraner, Robyn.
  The cat who wanted to fly.

  Summary: When Maggie the witch refuses to allow her
to fly, Midnight the cat decides to learn a spell of
her own.
  [1. Witches—Fiction. 2. Cats—Fiction]
I. Goodman, Joan E., ill. II. Title.
PZ7.S9652Cat   1986   [E]   85-14119
ISBN 0-8167-0612-3 (lib. bdg.)
ISBN 0-8167-0613-1 (pbk.)

10   9   8   7   6   5   4   3   2   1

The CAT WHO WANTED to FLY

There was once a witch named
Maggie. She lived in a tall stone
tower with a small black cat
called Midnight.

The tower had only one window
at the very, very top. There were
no doors. There was not even a
mouse-hole.

When the moon was high and
the stars were bright, Maggie
would jump on her broomstick
and fly off into the night.

Midnight was not allowed to fly.
She had to stay home. She was
lonesome. She was angry. She sat
on the edge of the window,
howling at her bad luck.

8

Poor Midnight.
She begged. She cried, saying,
"Take me with you. I want to
fly, too."
But Maggie wouldn't listen.

"You're much too small," she
said. "You'll fall off the broom
and break your silly neck."

"I won't," said Midnight.
"You will," said Maggie.
"I won't."
"You will."
"I won't!"
"BE STILL!"

When Maggie tried to pet her,
Midnight showed her claws.

Maggie just laughed. She pointed
a finger and said, "Toads and
spiders! Bats and doom!
Buttercups and daisies, *bloom!*"

When Midnight looked, her
claws were gone. Flowers grew
in their place.

"What a fine bouquet," said
Maggie. "Did you pick it for me?
What a nice little kitten you are."

Then she laughed and laughed.

Each night, Midnight dreamed
of flying—the clouds far below,
the wind whistling in her ears.

Sometimes she hid in Maggie's black hat. She closed her eyes and lay very still. *Maybe Maggie won't see me*, she thought.

But Maggie always did.
"No more tricks, you rascal, or
I'll turn you into a toad."

"Good," said Midnight. "I'd rather be a toad. I'd rather be anything than a cat who never flies!"

"Would you, my dear?" said
Maggie. "Would you indeed?"
And she snapped her fingers
three times.
One! Two! Three!

Midnight was wrong. She had to admit it. Being yourself, no matter how hard, was really best of all.

One day, just to get even,
Midnight broke all the jars on
Maggie's shelf. Newts and frogs
and slippery things went hopping
and wiggling all over the place.

Maggie was furious.
"So, my pet, you want to fly, do you? You'll fly," she cried. "You'll fly!"

Again she pointed her finger.

"Bats and birds and things that
fly—lift this cat up very high!"

At once, Midnight flew up to the
ceiling. Without even trying, she
sailed across the room.

She flew faster and faster,
around and around, until she
was so dizzy she begged Maggie
to lift the spell.

At last, Midnight fell to the floor
with a *bump!*
"Hee, hee, hee!" laughed
Maggie. "Haw, haw, haw!"

Laugh if you like, thought Midnight. She had an idea of her own.

From then on, when Maggie was out flying, Midnight stayed home and read. She learned about magic. She learned how to cast a spell. She read every book that Maggie owned. She even read some of them twice.

When she was very sure that
nothing could go wrong,
Midnight sat at the window and
waited for a full moon.
She did not have long to wait.

When the time was right and
Maggie was asleep, Midnight
found the magic feather she'd
been hiding.

Soft as a whisper, she tiptoed to
Maggie's bed and waved the
feather in the air three times.

Maggie snored. She muttered in
her sleep. She turned on her left
side. She turned on her right.
But soon she settled down again,
and everything was quiet.

Midnight raised the feather. She whispered the magic words, "Giggle, gaggle, google, gop! Laugh and laugh and *never* stop!"

Then Maggie began to laugh.

She laughed until the bed shook.
She laughed until she fell on the
floor.
"Haw, haw, haw!" she hollered.
"Ha, ha, ha!" she roared.

She laughed so hard, she couldn't stop. She laughed so hard, she couldn't speak. She laughed so hard, she couldn't break the spell.

"Let me fly!" said Midnight.
Maggie didn't answer.

"I'll be careful," Midnight promised. "I'll be good, and I won't try any tricks."

Maggie nodded her head. She
shook it up and down.
"Promise," said Midnight.

Maggie rolled her eyes. It was
the best she could do.
"All right," said Midnight, and
she lifted the spell.

Now you may not think so, but a witch's promise can never be broken.

So the next night, when the moon was high, Maggie climbed on her broomstick and Midnight climbed on, too.

Then, for the very first time,
with the stars all around her and
the clouds far below, Midnight
rode deep, deep into the night.

And the wind whistled in her
ears.